For Liam, Cash and all the Kings and Queens
who read this book. You make our lives an
adventure every day and we love you for it.
— Your Royal Caretakers

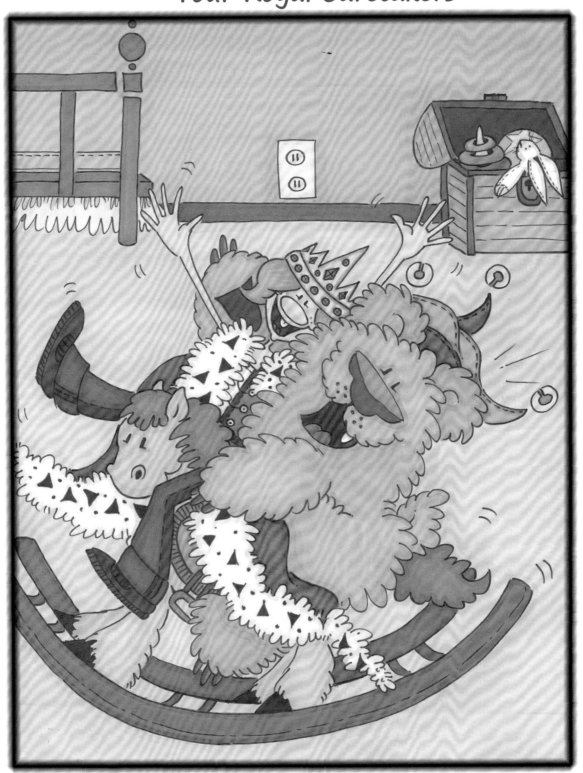

To my friends, family and especially Megan.
I thank God daily for your honesty, advice and support.
— N.D.

Hello, I'm "N" and this is "M"
and this...

...is King Boogie.

He is the King of the castle we live in
and we are his Royal Caretakers!

This is King Boogie's Big Blue Bear
which he named...

Bear!

King Boogie and Bear go everywhere together because they are the best of friends!

Every morning, King Boogie
wakes up and looks over his
kingdom from his royal tower.

When King Boogie is ready
to leave his tower

we have to carry him and Bear
down a long flight of stairs!

Once downstairs, King Boogie loves to start every day with his royal milk and breakfast...

He sure does make a mess!

After breakfast, King Boogie
loves to play music.
He's really quite good at it!

One of King Boogie's favorite things
to do after playing music

is to sit down and
read a good book...

When he can get away with it,
King Boogie loves to play with my phone!

Sometimes, King Boogie and Bear play tricks on me!

When the weather
is nice outside

King Boogie loves seeing birds,
squirrels and cats,
but his favorite animal...

...Is a dog!

And no matter where we are,
if King Boogie hears a song...

He starts dancing!

And we dance too!

At the end of a long, fun day,
King Boogie eats his royal veggies
and brushes his teeth...

And then we sit together
and watch his favorite show.

And after carrying King Boogie and
Bear back up to his Royal Tower...

...we tuck him and Bear in for the night,
turn off the light and say...

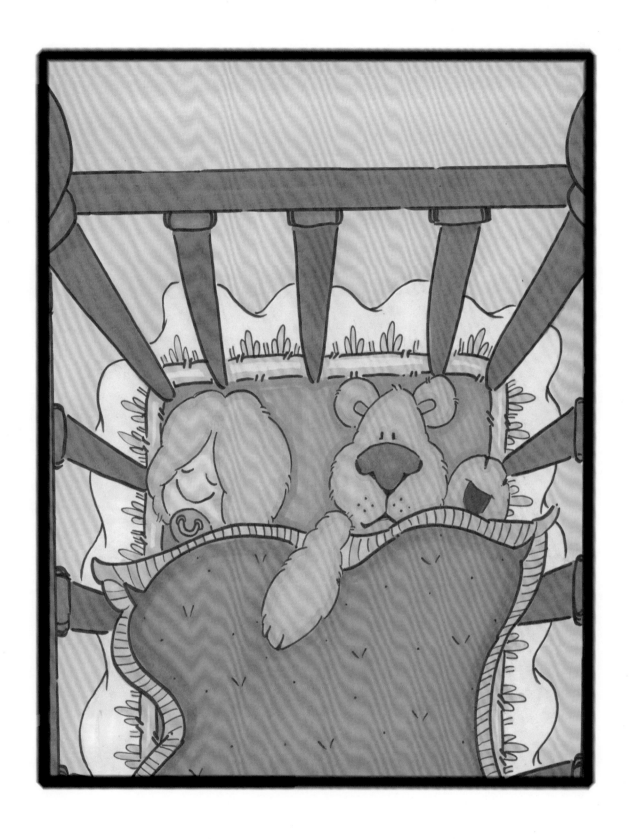

...'goodnight King Boogie,
we love you.'